Fitz-Greene Halleck

Young America

A Poem

Fitz-Greene Halleck

Young America
A Poem

ISBN/EAN: 9783743335158

Manufactured in Europe, USA, Canada, Australia, Japa

Cover: Foto ©Andreas Hilbeck / pixelio.de

Manufactured and distributed by brebook publishing software
(www.brebook.com)

Fitz-Greene Halleck

Young America

With face, like April's bright in smiles or
     tears,
His laugh a song—his step the forest deer's,
With heart as pure and liberal as the air,
And voice of sweetest tone, and bright gold hair
In thick curls clustering round his even brow,
And dimpled cheek—how calm he slumbers
     now !

—————

The sentry stars in heaven's blue above,
Sleep their sweet daybreak sleep, their watch
     withdrawn,
And lovely as a bride from dream of love,
Blushing and blooming, wakes the summer
     dawn ;
Winds—woods—and waters of the brook and
     bay

Wake at the fanning of the wings of day,

And birds and bells, in garden, tree, and tower,

Bow to the bidding of the wakening hour,

And breathe, the Hamlet's happy homes
    among

Morn's fragrant music from their lips of Song.

———

Within the loveliest of wayside bowers,

The summer home of loveliest leaves and
    flowers,

Cradled on rose-leaves, curtained round with
    vines,

And canopied by branches of a tree

Whose buds and blossoms charm the wander-
    ing bee,

In deep and dreaming sleep the youth re-
    clines.

Sunbeams, wind-cooled, their fond caressing
glow,

Twine, with leaf-shadows, the green roof be-
low,

In wedded love-clasp of sweet shade and light,

The enwoven harmony of the dark and bright,

And blend within, around it, and above,

Their balm, their bloom, their beauty, and
their joy,

Their watching—sleepless as the brooding
dove,

Their bounty—boundless as the fairy love

Of Queen Titania for her Henchman Boy.

————

II.

The doors are open in the house of prayer,
The morning worshippers are kneeling there
In supplicating harmony, beneath
The intoning organ's incense-bearing breath,
That aids their hymning voices, and around
Moves in the might and majesty of sound.
The pages of the Holy Book are read,
The solemn blessing of the Priest is said,
Departing footsteps gently press the floor,
And silence seals and guards the consecrated
    door.

Along his homeward pathway, lingering slow,

His dark weeds tokening a mourner's woe,

The Gospel-Teacher comes. The path in-
clines

His steps beside the cradle bower of vines

Where sleeps the boy. A moment's mute surprise,

And the mazed mourner greets, with grateful
eyes,

The enlivening presence of that cherub face,

Delighted in its loveliness to trace

The memorial beauty of his own lost boy,

A blossomed bud, death-doomed, in its spring-
time of joy;

And says, in whispers, "Would that I might
wake,

And woo, and win him, for his soul's sweet
    sake,

To make my home his cloister, and entwine

All his life's hopes and happiness with mine.

And with him win, dear daughter of the sky!

Handmaid of Heaven! immortal Piety!

Thy visitings, and joy to see thee bring

In sisterly embrace, wing folding wing,

Meek Faith, sweet Hope, and Charity divine,

With thee to consecrate that home a shrine

Among the holiest where the adorer kneels,

Listening the coming of thy chariot wheels.

Then the gay sportive dreams, enwreathing
    now

Their frolic fancies round the slumberer's
    brow,

1*

Should yield to dreams of angels entering in

His young heart's Eden, unprofaned by sin;

Then should his pleasant couch of leaves and
    flowers

Yield willing homage to the bliss of bowers

More beautiful than hers, and only givén

In visions of the scenery of Heaven;

Then should the music now around him heard,

The wind-harp's song, the song of bee and
    bird,

Yield to thy chorused carollings sublime,

And sky-endomed cathedral's chaunt and
    chime.

And then the longing of his life should be

To praise, to love, to worship thine and thee,

And when, my pastoral task of duty done,

I rest beneath the cold sepulchral stone,

Be his the delegated power to grace,

In surpliced sanctity, thy Altar place;

To feed thy chosen flock with heavenly food,

Be their kind Shepherd, gentle, generous, good,

And, in the language of the Minstrel's lay,

"Lure them to brighter worlds, and lead the way."

Hark! a bugle's echo comes,

Hark! a fife is singing,

Hark! the roll of far-off drums

Through the air is ringing!

————

The mourner turns—looks—listens, and is

gone,

In quiet heedlessness the Boy sleeps on.

————

III.

Nearer the bugle's echo comes,
  Nearer the fife is singing,
Near and more near the roll of drums
  Through the air is ringing.

War! it is thy music proud,
  Wakening the brave-hearted,
Memories—hopes—a glorious crowd,
  At its call have started.

Memories of our sires of old,
> Who, oppression-driven,
High their rainbow flag unrolled
> To the sun and sky of heaven.

Memories of the true and brave,
> Who, at Honor's bidding,
Stept, their Country's life to save,
> To war as to their wedding.

Memories of many a battle plain,
> Where, their life-blood flowing,
Made green the grass, and gold the grain,
> Above their grave-mounds growing.

Hopes—that the children of their prayers,
  With them in valor vieing,
May do as noble deeds as theirs,
  In living and in dying.

And make, for children yet to come,
  The land of their bequeathing
The imperial and the peerless home
  Of happiest beings breathing.

For this the warrior-path we tread,
  The battle-path of duty,
And change, for field and forest bed,
  Our bowers of love and beauty.

Music! bid thy minstrels play
No tunes of grief or sorrow,
Let them cheer the living brave to-day,
They may wail the dead to-morrow.

———

Such were the words, unvoiced by lip or
tongue,
The thought-enwoven themes, the mental song
Of One, high placed, beside the slumberer's
bower,
In the stern, silent chieftainship of power.

A War-king, seated on his saddle throne,

A listener to no counsels but his own,

The soldier leader of a soldier band,

Whose prescient skill, quick eye, and brief
    command,

Have won for him, on many a field of fame,

The immortality of a victor's name.

His troops, in thousands, now are marching
    by,

Heart-homage seen in each saluting eye,

And sword, and lance, and banner, bowing
    down

In tributary grace, before his bright renown.

And on, and on, as rank on rank appears,

Come, fast and loud, the thrice-repeated cheers

From voices of brave men whose life-long cry

Has been with him to live, for him to die.

Their plumes and pennons dancing in the
breeze,

With leaves and flowers of overarching trees,

Timing their steps to tunes of flute and fife,

And trump and drum, the joy of soldier life,

While o'er them wave, proud banner of the
free!

Thy sky-born stars and glorious colors three,

All beauteous in each interwoven hue

Of summer's rainbow, spanning earth and sea,

The rose's red and white, the violet's heavenly
blue,

Emblems of valor, purity and truth,

Long may they charm the air in ever-smiling
youth.

And now the rearmost files are hurrying by,

Closing the gorgeous scene of pomp and pa-
 geantry;

And far, far off, on wings of distance borne,

Speed the faint echoes of the trump and horn,

Plaintively breathing partings and farewells,

Solemn and sad as tones of tocsin bells,

But triumphed o'er by voices that prolong

The wild war music of the manlier song,

That bids the soldier's heart beat quick and
 gay,

The song of "O'er the hills and far away."

And now, beside the slumberer's couch of
leaves,
His parting web of thought the warrior chief-
tain weaves.

———

How sweetly the Boy in the beauty is sleep-
ing
Of Life's sunny morning of hope and of
youth,
May his guardian angels, their watch o'er him
keeping,
Keep his evening and noon in the pathways
of truth.

Ah me! what delight it would give me to
wake him,

And lead him wherever my life banners
wave,

O'er the pathways of glory and honor to take
him,

And teach him the lore of the bold and the
brave;

And when the war-clouds and their fierce
storm of water,

O'er the land that we love their outpourings
shall cease,

Bid him bear to her Ark, from her last field
   of slaughter,
  Upon Victory's wings, the green olive of
   Peace;

And when the death-note of my bugle has
   sounded,
  And memorial tears are embalming my
   name,
By young hearts like his may the grave be
   surrounded
  Where I sleep my last sleep in the sunbeams of fame.

———

Summoned to duty by his charger's neighs,

The only summons that his pride obeys,

He bows his farewell blessing, and is gone,

In quiet heedlessness the Boy sleeps on.

———

IV.

Merrily bounds the morning bark
Along the summer sea,
Merrily mounts the morning lark
The topmost twig on tree,

Merrily smiles the morning rose
    The morning sun to see,
And merrily, merrily greets the rose
    The honey-seeking bee.
But merrier, merrier far are these,
Who bring, on the wings of the morning
        breeze,
    A music sweeter than her own,
A happy group of loves and graces,
Graceful forms and lovely faces,
    All in gay delight outflown;
Outflown from their school-room cages,
School-room rules, and school-room pages,
Lovely in their teens and tresses,
Summer smiles, and summer dresses,

2

Joyous in their dance and song,

With sweet sisterly caresses,

Arm in arm they speed along;

" (Now pursuing, now retreating,

Now in circling troops they meet,

To brisk notes in cadence beating,

Glance their many twinkling feet.

Slow melting strains their Queen's approach

declare.

Where'er she turns the Graces homage pay,

With arms sublime, that float upon the air,)"

She comes—the gentle Lady of my Lay,

Well pleased that, for her welcome to prepare,

I borrow music from the Muse of Gray.

His heroine was the lovely Paphian Queen,

Mine seems the Huntress of the Sylvan scene,

The chaste Diana, with her Nymphs, in gay

And graceful beauty keeping holiday.

Sudden she pauses in the race of joy,

Around the Cradle Bower where sleeps the
	Boy,

And, with a sunny smile of gladness, sees

His golden ringlets, on the dancing breeze,

Shading his eyelids—and, with quick delight,

Bids her wild nymphs to wing their merry
	flight

Home to their morning nests, and leave her
	care

To watch the slumberer in his rose-leafed
	chair.

He, in his beauty, to her fancy seems
To be the young Endymion of her dreams
Of yester evening, when, alone and still,
Waiting the coming of the whip-poor-will,
Our climate's nightingale, her garden bird,
From lips unseen, unknown, this whispered
    song she heard:

———

" The summer winds are wandering here,
   In mountain freshness, pure and free,
And all that to the eye are dear
   In rock and torrent, flower and tree,

Upon the gazing stranger come,

    Till, in his starlight dreams at even,

It seems another Eden-home,

    Reared by the word—the breath of Heaven.

To-morrow—and the stranger's gone,

    And other scenes, as bright as this,

May win it from his bosom soon,

    And dim its wild-wood loveliness.

But ever round this spot his heart

    Will be—while Memory's leaves are green,

The fairy scene may be forgot,

    But not the Fairy of the scene.

The song she sang, the lip that breathed it,

　　The cheek of rose, the speaking eye,

The brow of snow, the hair that wreathed it,

　　In their young life and purity,

Will dwell within his heart among

　　His holiest, longest cherished things,

Themes worthy of a worthier song,

　　Dear Lady of the mountain springs."

———

And who is she—the Fairy of the scene?
A bright-eyed, beautiful maiden of eighteen,
Lovely and learnéd, and well "skilled to
    rule,"
The Lady-Mentor of a village school,
"Teaching young Girls' ideas how to shoot;"
A tree of knowledge, rich in flowers and fruit,
A model heroine in mien and mind,
An "Admirable Crichton" crinolined,
And author of a charming Book that sings
Delightfully concerning wedding rings,
Tracing the progress of the lightning dart
Between the bridal finger and the heart,
And proving the arithmetic untrue
Which teaches us that one and one make two,

Whereas the marriage ring is worn to prove

That two are one—the Algebra of Love.

Such is the Lady of my song, and now

She gazes on her young Endymion's brow,

And, fancying—by a sudden thought be-
guiled,

Herself a mother bending o'er her child,

Unconsciously imprints upon his eyes

A kiss—brimfull of all the charities,

Sacredly secret, eloquently mute,

Yet "musical as is Apollo's lute,"

Of power to lure a swan from off the lake,

Or wooing blue-bird from an April tree,

Upsprings the Boy, exclaiming, I'm awake!

And shakes his golden locks in frolic glee.

One look—and, like an arrow from the string,

Away the maiden went, on laughing wing,

Graciously leaving, ere she homeward flew,

On the green turf impearled with drops of
dew,

Farewell impressions.of the prettiest foot

That ever graced and charmed a Gaiter Boot.

2*

V.

The awakened Boy, not fond of early rising,
Resumed his pillow, thus soliloquizing:

" That Lady's pleasant smile and ruby lip
Might hope to win my heart's companionship,
But for the memory of that morn which proved
    proved
That he is happiest who has never loved.

That morn, when I, within a Lady's bower,

Offered my heart, hand, and a handsome
dower

To ONE who, to my great and sad surprise,

Told me, with mischief in her laughing eyes,

That she was not at all inclined to marry,

And added, in a most provoking tone,

That YOUNG AMERICA had better ' tarry

At Jericho until his beard was grown,'

And like his Eagle, wear upon his wings

Feathers—before he proffered wedding rings;

That purpling grapes looked lovely on their
vines,

But she preferred them perfected in wines,

That on my cheek the down was fair to see,

But she admired the full-blown *favoris,*

And rather liked in men a modest pride
Of moustache—if artistically dyed."

She then, dismissing me in queenly state,
Locked of her Eden the unfeeling gate,
And I—a victim to Love's cruel dart,
Went—to the Opera—with a broken heart!

Along thy peopled solitude—Broadway!
I walked, a desolate man; day after day,
With downcast eyes and melancholy brow,
    Until a lady's letter asked me why
I passed her ladyship without a bow;

To which I sent the following reply,
My earliest-born attempt at poetry:

————

" The heart hath sorrows of its own,
    And griefs it veils from all,
  And tears, close-hidden from the world,
    In solitude will fall,
  And when its thoughts of agony
    Upon the bosom lie,
Even Beauty in her loveliness
    May pass unheeded by.

" 'Tis only on the happy
    That she never looks in vain,
  To them her smiles are rainbow hopes,
    New-born of summer rain,
  And their glad hearts will worship her,
    As one whose home is heaven;
  A being of a brighter world,
    To earth a season given.

" That time with me has been and gone,
    And life's best music now
  Is but the winter's wind that bends
    The leafless forest bough.

And I would shun, if that could be,
    The light of young blue eyes,
They bring back hours I would forget,
    And painful memories.

" Yet, lady, though too few and brief,
    There are bright moments still,
When I can free my prisoned thoughts,
    And wing them where I will,
And then thy smiles come o'er my heart
    Like sunbeams o'er the sea,
And I can bow as once I bowed
    When all was well with me."

And now farewell to Rhyme! and welcome
    Reason!

'Tis past—my early manhood's pleasant sea-
    son;

If morning dreams, that visit our closed eyes,

Changed, when we wake to Life's realities,

I might become a SOLDIER of renown,

Or wear a PREACHER's or a TEACHER's gown;

For all three in my dreams since rose the sun,

Have sought to make me their adopted one,

Destined to run the race that each has run;

But my Ambition's leaves no more are green,

In one brief month my age will be FIFTEEN.

I've seen the world, and by the world been
    seen,

And now am speeding fast upon the way

To the calm, quiet evening of my day;

There but remains one promise to fulfil,

I bow myself obedient to its will,

And am prepared to settle down in life

By wooing—winning—wedding A Rich Wife.